A Light in the Forest

Written by
John Townsend

Illustrated by
Dynamo

Winter came to the forest. The nights grew darker and colder. Danger deepened. Shadows hid pits that could swallow a bear. Ice crusted over ponds that could crack and gulp anyone down.

When the moon was hidden by clouds, the forest was darker than down a tiger's throat. This was the time when the snow-wolf came down from the hills, prowling for food. It would hunt in the forest for someone to eat. Anyone.

Rabbits trembled in their burrows.

Badgers dug deeper into their setts.

Deer huddled timidly in caves.

A howl filled the forest. The hungry snow-wolf was on the prowl. Everyone shivered as they listened for the soft crunch in the snow. They feared the pad of the snow-wolf's feet. They dreaded the panting of its steamy breath in the frosty air.

"We can't go on like this," King Stag said. "Where is the moon to help us see in the forest?"

"Don't worry," said the wise old snowy owl. "A light is on its way. I've flown beyond the distant hills and I have seen wonderful things."

That night the snow fell like never before. The icy wind howled through the trees and heavy clouds covered the moon, hiding its glow.

At midnight a tiny light appeared in the sky. It winked and blinked as it moved over the treetops.

"Is that a star?" a badger snorted, as it blinked up at the twinkling light.

White wings shone in a shimmering light. The snowy owl swept silently down through the trees.

In its talons it gripped a jar with a burning candle inside. The light danced and sparkled on the glinting snow.

"How wonderful," sighed the dormouse.

"I'm not so sure," said King Stag. "This could be a trick."

"A trick of the light?" grinned the fox.

"Great news," Snowy Owl said. "This light is for all of us. Always."

"What good will that be?" a rat grumbled. "We want the moon. We need the light of the moon."

"The sun would be better," everyone shouted. They all turned their backs on the light and returned to their gloomy dens.

Dormouse and Snowy Owl were left in the pool of golden light.

"I thought they'd be pleased," Snowy Owl said sadly.

Dormouse sighed. "That light could change our lives. After all, without it you would pounce on me and gobble me up. But now, as we share this golden glow together, we are friends."

"How right you are. So it's up to us to show the others."

The owl went round the whole forest, offering the light to everyone. No one wanted it. "We prefer things as they are," they all said.

The snow-wolf returned in the dead of night. Everyone froze at the sound: the soft crunch of the snow-wolf's feet.

Nearer and nearer it came. Crunch … crunch … crunch.

A goose laid an egg in panic. A hedgehog rolled into a ball. Crunch … crunch … crunch.

Howls echoed around the forest. No one slept a wink.

In the morning they all saw the footprints … and the snow stained red.

King Stag sighed. "This would never have happened if we had used the light. We'd have seen the snow-wolf coming."

"That's why we all need each other," Dormouse beamed. "If we work together, instead of hiding away in our dark little holes alone, we can make a BIG difference!"

Dormouse gathered twigs to pile up in the clearing. "Will you all add what you can to my pile?"

Grumbles and mumbles rumbled and tumbled through the forest. But, one by one, each animal added to the pile.

Rabbits fetched straw and dry leaves.

Squirrels brought heaps of nutshells.

Badgers dug up chunks of peat.

Deer dragged branches and broken antlers.

Birds collected old nests and beavers piled up logs.

Everyone brought whatever they had. Soon they all stood around a tower in the middle of the forest.

That night the snow-wolf returned. An icy howl filled the night. The animals froze at the soft crunch of the snow-wolf's feet.

Nearer and nearer it came. Crunch … crunch … crunch.

Snowy Owl swooped to the foot of the towering pile and put the light to the dry twigs.

Fizz … crackle … rustle … hiss … woooooosh!

Sparkle … flicker … twinkle … flash … WOWWWW!

The light flared and glared and blazed and dazzled as the fire took hold.

The forest lit up and everyone's eyes shone in the brilliant glow.

The night was filled with cheers, as the yelping snow-wolf ran like the wind back to the hills – never to return.

Snowy Owl smiled. "We will take it in turns to keep the flame burning, so the light never goes out. We will share it together – forever!"

For the first time ever, everyone agreed.

The forest has never been the same since.

Fear vanished with a burst of blazing brightness.

With everyone working together, the light still shines in the darkness.

The darkness has never put it out.